Richard Scarry's
BEST HOUSE EVER

Originally published as *Mouse's House*

Text by Kathryn and Byron Jackson • Illustrated by Richard Scarry

A GOLDEN BOOK • NEW YORK
Western Publishing Company, Inc., Racine, Wisconsin 53404

Two little mice once lived in a small red sock in a garden. Frisker, who liked to stay warm, slept in the heel. Her husband, Whisker, a brave little mouse who was very fond of fresh air, slept in the toe. There was a little hole in the toe, just the right size for a mouse's window.

Between the two mice there was just enough room for a bag full of sunflower seeds. Frisker and Whisker were always nibbling at the seeds. Before long there was not one seed left in the bag.

"We'll have to go shopping," said Frisker. Frisker took her basket and Whisker grabbed his hat, and the two mice set out for the store.

Soon after they were gone, a fluffy gray kitten scampered into the garden. "It's nearly winter," the kitten said to herself. "I wish I had a woolen hat to keep my ears warm."

Just then she saw the small red sock. "The very thing I need!" she exclaimed.

The kitten picked up the sock
and dumped out the mice's things.
She tied a knot in the toe and
pulled the sock over her head. It
fitted perfectly. The kitten was
very happy with her new red hat.

When the mice came back and
saw that their house was gone,
Frisker began to cry.

"Don't cry," begged Whisker.
"I'll find a better house."

He scurried about, sniffing and searching, until he found a little green pocketbook, all lined with silk. Frisker stopped crying the moment she saw it.

"It will make a wonderful house," she said with a smile.

In no time at all, the mice moved into their new house. It was cozy and warm. But the first time they went out for a walk, a fuzzy yellow duckling came waddling into the garden.

"When I have eggs," the duckling
thought, "I'm not going to sit, sit, sit on
a nest all day like my mother." Then she
saw the little green pocketbook. The
duckling let out a joyful quack, picked
up the purse, and waddled home.

"I can't wait to show Mother
how I'm going to carry my eggs
around with me," she said.

When the mice came back and found their green house gone, even Whisker felt like crying. But he was a brave little mouse, so he went off through the long grass to search for another house.

Before long he came back, looking very proud.

"I've found the best house yet," Whisker said. It was a small blue muff, the kind a young girl might use to keep her hands warm. It had velvet on the outside and fur on the inside. The mice curled up in the muff and quickly fell asleep.

Soon a red puppy came running into the garden. When he saw the velvety muff, he sniffed at it and smiled.

The muff smelled sweet and mousy, and it felt wonderfully soft. "This will make a fine pillow," the puppy said.

The puppy grabbed the muff with his teeth and shook it. The two little mice tumbled out of the muff and fell to the ground. They were shaking with fright.

"There goes our blue house," whispered Whisker as the red puppy disappeared into the bushes with the muff.

"I'll find an even better house," Whisker said bravely. Then he saw the gray kitten strolling into the yard, wearing the red sock on her head.

"So that's where our red house went," said Frisker. She started to cry.

"Don't cry," Whisker said. "I'll find the best house ever." And off he went to search the garden.

Soon he came scampering back. "I've found the best house you ever did see," he said.

When Frisker saw the house, she squealed with joy. This was a real house with a chimney and a door and windows with real curtains. It was a dollhouse that had been left under a rosebush and forgotten. It was just the right size for two little mice.

But the house was dusty and needed painting. Frisker and Whisker got to work. They washed the windows and curtains, swept the floors, made the beds, and built a fire in the tiny fireplace. Frisker prepared a delicious lunch of pumpkin-seed pie and tea.

The two little mice had just sat down at their table, all ready to eat, when they heard a loud quacking noise.

The fuzzy yellow duckling had seen the house, too. She tried to get in through the door, but it was locked. Then she tried to get in through the upstairs windows, but she couldn't get them open.

So the yellow duckling flew onto the roof and tried to squeeze
down the chimney.

"This is our house," said Frisker angrily.

The duckling just laughed. So Whisker blew at the fire with a little
bellows, and thick smoke rose up the chimney. The smoke made
the duckling sneeze and cough and made her eyes sting, too.

She flew away, choking and wiping her eyes.

"No one is going to take this house away from us," Whisker said bravely.

The minute lunch was over, the two mice began working again. Whisker helped Frisker in the kitchen. They baked pies, cakes, tarts, puddings, and rolls and set them on the table to cool.

"Now we'll rake the lawn and paint the shutters," Whisker said.

He and Frisker worked so hard that they didn't see or hear the gray kitten come creeping into the garden until she was almost upon them.

"Run," cried Whisker when he saw the kitten.

The two little mice scurried into the house in such a hurry that they forgot to lock the door.

They hid in the dish cupboard just in time. The minute they were inside, the front door opened, and the kitten peeped in.

The kitten purred happily when she saw the table full of all the good things that Frisker and Whisker had baked. The kitten squeezed into the house, pulled the sock off her head, and hung it on the doorknob. She sat down at the table and quickly gobbled up all the pies, cakes, tarts, puddings, and rolls.

This made Whisker so angry that he jumped up and down in a terrible rage. When he did, down came the cupboard shelf, with dishes, glasses, and even Frisker and Whisker. Everything fell to the floor with a loud bang.

The noise frightened the kitten, and she ran toward the door. But on the way out she got her paw tangled up in the red sock hanging on the doorknob. Then the door slammed on her tail. Meowing loudly, the kitten freed her tail and ran away.

Whisker and Frisker ran to the door and locked it. But as they
turned the key they heard a loud "Bow-wow-wow" outside.
"Let me in," said the red puppy.
"Oh, no, we won't," cried the two mice. "Go away."

But the puppy wouldn't go away. He pushed up the window and was about to climb in when the window slipped and fell down on his paw. The puppy yelped in pain.

"Serves him right," cried Frisker.

But the puppy howled so sadly that Frisker and Whisker pushed up the window and set him free.

"Thanks," said the puppy. "If anyone ever bothers you again, just tell me and I'll help you."

"Our troubles are over," said Whisker happily.

The two mice joined hands and danced around their new house.

The little gray kitten was sitting at home in her soft basket, thinking of the delicious lunch she had eaten at the mouse house.

"Maybe I'll go back there," she thought.

She put on her red stocking hat and then took it off as she remembered the door slamming on her tender tail. She decided never to go anywhere near the mouse house again.

The fuzzy yellow duckling was paddling around her pond, thinking about the mouse house.

"It is a lovely house," she said. "I would certainly like to live there myself."

Then she remembered the choking smoke and decided that her nice cool duck pond was a better place to live. And she never went back to the mouse house again.

The red puppy stopped in once a week just to make sure that Whisker and Frisker were safe and sound. He was glad to hear that no one ever bothered them.

After his visits the puppy would return to his doghouse. There he slept soundly on his fine velvet muff pillow, which smelled sweet and mousy and was wonderfully soft.

Whisker and Frisker felt safe and happy in their new house.
Before long they had four baby mice. The baby mice slept in four
little cradles Whisker had found in the attic.

Every night, just before bedtime, Whisker walked through the house, gazing proudly at each room.

"I told you I'd find a house that was just right for us," he told Frisker.

Frisker smiled at her husband. "This is the best house ever," she said.